South Huntington Public Library
145 Pidgeon Hill Road
Huntington Station, NY 11746

Colin Kaepernick

By David Aretha

Consultant: Barry Wilner
AP Football Writer

New York, New York

Credits

Cover and Title Page, © Greg Trott/AP Images, Aaron Kehoe/AP Images, and Alison Yin/McDonald's USA/AP Images; 4, © Hector Amezcua/The Sacramento Bee/AP Images; 5, © Hector Amezcua/The Sacramento Bee/AP Images; 6, © Seth Poppel/Yearbook Library; 7T, © Seth Poppel/Yearbook Library; 7B, © Seth Poppel/Yearbook Library; 8, © Seth Poppel/Yearbook Library; 9, © David Godinez/Cal Sport Media/Newscom; 10, © Dean Hare/AP Images; 11, © Marcio Jose Sanchez/AP Images; 12, © Robin Alam/Icon Sportswire; 13, © Greg Trott/AP Images; 14, © Marcio Jose Sanchez/AP Images; 15, © Dave Martin/AP Images; 16, © Marty Bicek/ZUMA Press/Corbis; 17, © Marty Bicek/ZUMA Press/Corbis; 18, © Marty Bicek/ZUMA Press/Corbis; 19, © Marty Bicek/ZUMA Press/Corbis; 20, © Andy Alfaro/ZUMA Press/Newscom; 21, © Greg Trott/AP Images; 22L, © Staff/MCT/Newscom; 22R, © Hector Amezcua/The Sacramento Bee/AP Images.

Publisher: Kenn Goin
Editor: Jessica Rudolph
Creative Director: Spencer Brinker
Photo Researcher: Chrös McDougall
Design: Dawn Beard Creative

Library of Congress Cataloging-in-Publication Data in process at time of publication (2015)
Library of Congress Control Number: 2014036643
ISBN-13: 978-1-62724-544-9 (library binding)

Copyright © 2015 Bearport Publishing Company, Inc. All rights reserved. No part of this publication may be reproduced in whole or in part, stored in any retrieval system, or transmitted in any form or by any means, electronic, mechanical, photocopying, recording, or otherwise, without written permission from the publisher.

For more information, write to Bearport Publishing Company, Inc., 45 West 21st Street, Suite 3B, New York, New York 10010. Printed in the United States of America.

10 9 8 7 6 5 4 3 2 1

CONTENTS

Man on the Run 4
A Young Talent 6
Football over Baseball 8
Speedy and Accurate 10
A Childhood Dream 12
A Star Is Born 14
A Warm Heart 16
Happy Campers 18
Another Great Run 20

The Colin File 22
Glossary 23
Bibliography 24
Read More 24
Learn More Online 24
Index 24

Man on the Run

On January 12, 2013, San Francisco 49ers quarterback Colin Kaepernick took a snap to start a play. His team was tied 24–24 with the Green Bay Packers in a **playoff** game. Most quarterbacks would pass the ball or hand it off to a teammate. Colin, however, is no ordinary quarterback. He faked a handoff and **sprinted** down the field with the ball. Colin ran 56 yards (51 m) for a touchdown! The 49ers took the lead and went on to win the game 45–31.

Colin's **rushing** game was a key part of the 49ers' win. The team even reached the Super Bowl that year. Football fans everywhere were buzzing about the exciting young quarterback.

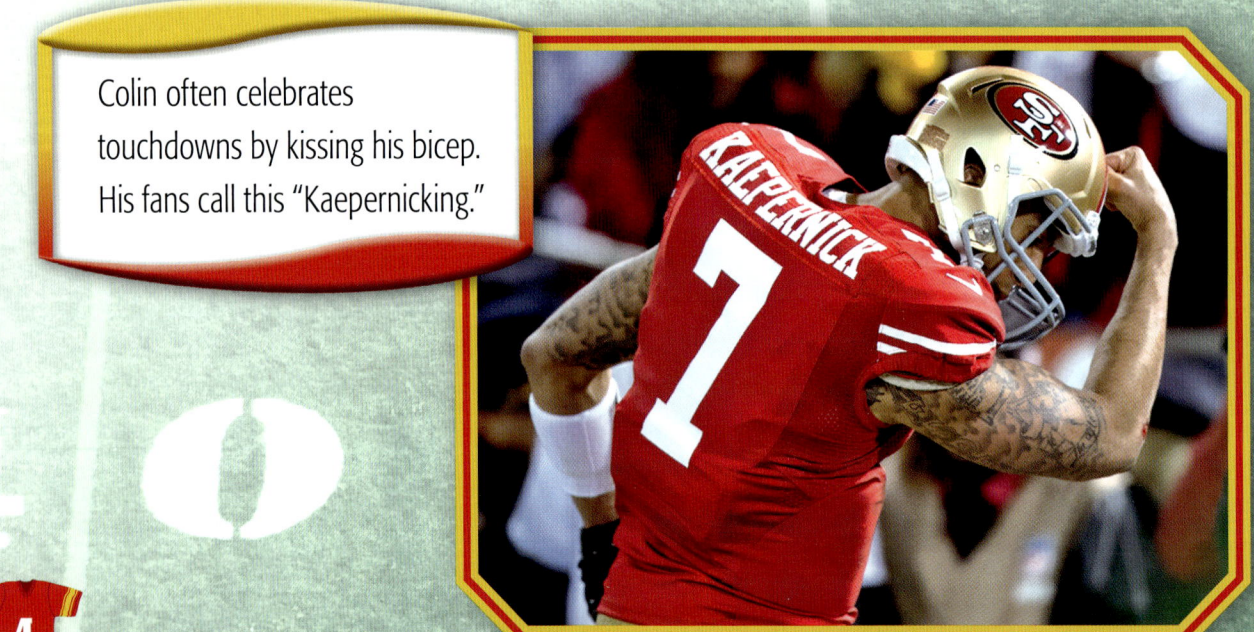

Colin often celebrates touchdowns by kissing his bicep. His fans call this "Kaepernicking."

During the game against the Packers, Colin set an all-time record for a quarterback rushing in an NFL game, with 181 yards (166 m).

A Young Talent

Colin was born in Wisconsin on November 3, 1987. His father left the family, and his mother could not take care of a baby by herself. So, she allowed Rick and Teresa Kaepernick to **adopt** Colin.

The new family soon moved to California. As a child, Colin loved to play football. By age nine, he was the quarterback for his youth team. Young quarterbacks often struggle to throw long passes, but not Colin. "He had an extremely strong arm," his mother said.

Colin wasn't great at just football. His speed and strong arm made him stand out in many sports. In high school, Colin was a star player on the football, basketball, and baseball teams.

Colin as a baby

Colin has a brother and a sister. His parents, Rick and Teresa, had two other children, both boys, who passed away from **heart defects** when they were babies.

Colin played football, baseball, and basketball at John H. Pitman High School in Turlock, California.

Colin playing football in high school

Football over Baseball

In high school, Colin was a fantastic **pitcher** on his baseball team. He could fire fastballs at 94 miles per hour (151 kph), and he even threw two **no-hitters**. By the end of high school, many colleges offered him baseball **scholarships**. However, Colin had his heart set on football, so he turned down the baseball scholarships.

Colin hoped a college would offer him a football scholarship, but most football coaches were not interested in him. They thought he was too skinny and would get injured by bigger players. They also didn't like the form he used to throw the football. Only one **FBS** school offered Colin a football scholarship—the University of Nevada. Colin gladly accepted the offer.

Colin was a good student in high school. He got mostly A's on his report cards.

Colin avoids being tackled during a 2011 game for the University of Nevada.

In high school, Colin made a videotape of his best plays on the football field. He sent copies of the tape to approximately 100 college teams. Still, only Nevada was interested in Colin.

Speedy and Accurate

The University of Nevada head football coach saw that Colin had a talent few other quarterbacks had. He could run—fast! Opponents struggled to keep up with Colin and tackle him.

However, Colin wanted to one day play in the NFL. To do so, he knew he would need to become a more accurate passer. He had a strong arm but couldn't always get the ball directly to his teammates. Colin worked with his coaches on his accuracy, and it paid off. He became the first college quarterback to rush for 1,000 yards (914 m) and pass for 2,000 yards (1,829 m) in three different seasons.

Colin's best college game was in 2010 against the University of Idaho. He threw for five touchdowns in a 63–17 win.

Colin (right) runs with the ball against Idaho in 2010.

Colin improved his passing skills during college.

A Childhood Dream

In 2011, Colin entered the NFL **draft**. He was thrilled when the San Francisco 49ers chose him. The Niners were wowed by Colin's strength, speed, and hard-working attitude.

The 49ers already had an excellent **starting** quarterback in Alex Smith. So, Colin began his career as a **backup**. That was okay, though, because he had a lot to learn. Many young quarterbacks need at least one season to get used to the faster, more complicated NFL game. Colin played in only three games that first season. Then he came into the next season still backing up Alex.

Colin (left) and Alex Smith

During his first NFL season, Colin played very little and only threw five passes.

Playing for the 49ers had been Colin's childhood dream. In fourth grade, he wrote a letter to his future self that read, "I hope I go to a good college in football, then go to the pros and play on the Niners or the Packers."

A Star Is Born

Everything changed for Colin in November 2012, after Alex Smith got injured during a game. Colin started in the next game, against the Chicago Bears. He wowed fans by passing for 243 yards (222 m) and two touchdowns. The 49ers easily won 32–7.

The Niners' coach decided to keep Colin as the starter even after Alex got better. It was the right decision. That year, Colin led his team to the Super Bowl, against the Baltimore Ravens. It was a close game. However, San Francisco's last **drive** ended on Baltimore's 5-yard (4.6 m) line. The Ravens won 34–31. Fans were still amazed, though. In just his second season, Colin had almost led the 49ers to a Super Bowl victory.

Colin celebrates after the win over the Bears.

Colin **completed** 12 of his first 15 passes against the Bears in the November 2012 game.

Colin runs into the end zone for a touchdown during Super Bowl XLVII (47) in 2013.

A Warm Heart

When Colin became a pro football player, he started to make a lot of money. His first thought was to use some of his money to help others. He especially wanted to help kids with heart defects.

Heart defects, like the ones that had killed Colin's two brothers, are a big problem for many children. Each year in the United States, 40,000 babies are born with heart defects. Living a healthy life can be a struggle for many of those who survive. Colin learned about a camp in Salida, California, where kids with heart problems can enjoy outdoor activities. It's called Camp Taylor. Since 2011, Colin has donated money to Camp Taylor. He also spends a great deal of time with the campers.

Colin stands with Camp Taylor kids.

Colin (top center) poses with kids during a visit to Jessica's House in Turlock, California.

Colin also supports Jessica's House. The organization provides support for kids who are grieving from a death in the family.

17

Happy Campers

Camp Taylor is important to Colin because he knows that kids with heart defects often feel left out. They might want to run around with their healthier friends but can't keep up because of their **condition**. The camp offers activities that children who struggle with heart problems can safely do together. Campers enjoy everything from swimming to horseback riding. "It's an amazing experience being with a bunch of kids with heart disease just like myself," said one camper.

When Colin visits Camp Taylor, the kids burst into smiles. He laughs with the campers. He plays football with them. "He's a kid magnet," said Kimberlie Gamino, the **founder** of Camp Taylor. "The kids flock to him."

A Camp Taylor camper hugs Colin in 2013.

Camp Taylor activities also include snorkeling, rock-wall climbing, face painting, and much more.

The kids at Camp Taylor love it when Colin visits them.

Another Great Run

Many opponents have tried to stop Colin's passing and running game, but few have succeeded. In the 2013–2014 season, Colin again led the 49ers to the playoffs. After that, the 49ers knew they had one of the most talented NFL quarterbacks. So, they signed Colin to play with the team for another six years.

Niners fans were happy, and so was Colin. He loves playing for the 49ers, but he loves helping people even more. Reporters have asked what he will do with the additional money he'll be making in the NFL. He is quick to answer that Camp Taylor "will be getting another check."

A group of Camp Taylor kids with Colin at an event to raise money for the camp

Colin makes a pass during a 2014 playoff game against the Seattle Seahawks.

In the 2014 **NFC Championship Game** against the Seattle Seahawks, Colin made the longest run ever by a quarterback in an NFL playoff game. It was 58 yards (53 m)!

The Colin File

Colin is a football hero on and off the field. Here are some highlights.

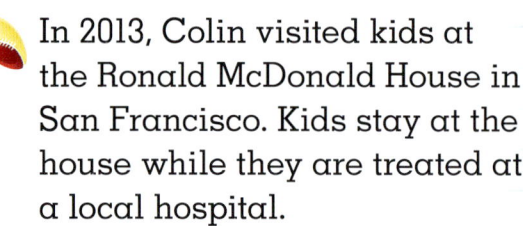

- In fourth grade, Colin wrote, "I think in seven years I will be between six feet to six feet four inches, 140 pounds." He grew to be six feet four inches (1.9 m). He weighs 230 pounds (104 kg).

- Colin owns a tortoise named Sammy. The 100-pound (45 kg) creature has his own 49ers jersey with his name on it. Colin drapes the jersey over his shell.

- In 2013, Colin visited kids at the Ronald McDonald House in San Francisco. Kids stay at the house while they are treated at a local hospital.

- Colin didn't play baseball in college, but professional baseball teams were still interested in him as a pitcher. In 2009, the Chicago Cubs drafted him. However, Colin decided to continue playing football at the University of Nevada.

Glossary

adopt (uh-DOPT) to take into one's family

backup (BAK-uhp) a player who doesn't play at the start of a game and often doesn't play at all; the second-best player in a position

completed (kuhm-PLEE-tid) achieved a pass that was successfully caught by a receiver

condition (kuhn-DISH-uhn) a long-term health problem

draft (DRAFT) an event in which professional teams take turns choosing college athletes to play for them

drive (DRIVE) a series of plays in which the team with the ball tries to move down the field

FBS (EFF-BEE-ESS) Football Bowl Subdivision; the highest level of college football, in which the top 120 teams play

founder (FOUN-dur) the person who creates an organization, company, or school

heart defects (HART DEE-fekts) problems in the structure of the heart

NFC Championship Game (EN-EFF-SEE CHAMP-ee-uhn-ship GAYM) the final playoff game in the National Football Conference (NFC); the winner goes to the Super Bowl to face the AFC (American Football Conference) winner

no-hitters (noh-HIT-turz) baseball games in which a pitcher does not allow batters from the other team to get a base hit

pitcher (PICH-ur) a player on a baseball team who throws to the batter to start each play

playoff (PLAY-awf) a postseason period in which the best regular-season teams compete against each other to determine who will go to the Super Bowl

rushing (RUHSH-ing) the act of running with the football

scholarships (SKOL-ur-ships) money given to people so they can go to college

sprinted (SPRINT-id) ran at full speed for a short distance

starting (START-ing) playing at the start of a game; being the best player at a position

Bibliography

Himmelsbach, Adam. "Not a Household Name, Not Even in Nevada." *The New York Times* (August 28, 2010).

Vanderbeek, Brian. "Turlock's Kaepernick Ecstatic Over Being Picked by 49ers." *The Modesto Bee* (August 29, 2011).

www.49ers.com

www.kidsheartcamp.org

Read More

Hoblin, Paul. *Colin Kaepernick (Playmakers)*. Minneapolis, MN: ABDO (2014).

Whiting, Jim. *The Story of the San Francisco 49ers (NFL Today)*. Mankato, MN: Creative Education (2014).

Yomtov, Nel. *Colin Kaepernick (Football Stars Up Close)*. New York: Bearport (2014).

Learn More Online

To learn more about Colin Kaepernick and the San Francisco 49ers, visit www.bearportpublishing.com/FootballHeroes

Index

Baltimore Ravens 14
baseball 6–7, 8, 22
basketball 6–7
Camp Taylor 16, 18–19, 20
Chicago Bears 14
Chicago Cubs 22
family 6, 16
Gamino, Kimberlie 18

Green Bay Packers 4–5, 13
heart defects 6, 16, 18
Jessica's House 17
John H. Pitman High School 7, 8–9
Ronald McDonald House 22
Salida, California 16

San Francisco 49ers 4, 12–13, 14, 20, 22
Seattle Seahawks 21
Smith, Alex 12, 14
Super Bowl 4, 14–15
Turlock, California 7, 17
University of Idaho 10
University of Nevada 8–9, 10
Wisconsin 6

16 99